W9-DDJ-978

DoG BReath

THE HoRRible Trouble WiTH Hally Tosis

DAV Pilkey

SCHOLASTIC INC.

New York Toronto London Auckland Sydney
Mexico City New Delhi Hong Kong Buenos Aires

For Mom and Dad and Halle

No part of this publication may be reproduced, stored in a
retrieval system, or transmitted in any form or by any means,
electronic, mechanical, photocopying, recording, or otherwise,
without written permission of the publisher. For information regarding
permission, write to Scholastic Inc., Attention: Permissions Department,
557 Broadway, New York, NY 10012.

This book was originally published in hardcover by the Blue Sky Press in 1994.

ISBN-13: 978-0-439-59839-2
ISBN-10: 0-439-59839-7

Copyright © 1994 by Dav Pilkey

All rights reserved. Published by Scholastic Inc.
SCHOLASTIC, THE BLUE SKY PRESS, and associated logos are
trademarks and/or registered trademarks of Scholastic Inc.

12 11 10 9   9 10 11 12/0

Printed in the U.S.A.   40
First Bookshelf edition, June 2004

here once was a dog named Hally,
who lived with the Tosis family.
Hally Tosis was a very good dog,
but she had a big problem.

Hally Tosis had horrible breath.
Whenever Hally Tosis opened her mouth,
horrible things happened.

When the children took Hally Tosis
for a walk, everyone else walked

on the other side of the street.
Even skunks avoided Hally Tosis.

But the real trouble started one day
when Grandma Tosis stopped by
for a cup of tea...

. . . and Hally jumped up to say hello.

Mr. and Mrs. Tosis were not amused. "Something has to be done about that smelly dog," they said.

The next day, Mr. and Mrs. Tosis
decided to find a new home for Hally.

The children knew that the only way
they could save their dog was to get
rid of her bad breath. So they took
Hally Tosis to the top of a mountain
that had a breathtaking view.

They hoped that the breathtaking view
would take Hally's breath away...

. . . but it didn't.

Next, the children took Hally Tosis
to a very exciting movie.

They hoped that all the excitement
would leave Hally breathless...

. . . but it didn't.

Finally, the children took Hally Tosis to a carnival. They hoped that Hally would lose her breath on the speedy roller coaster...

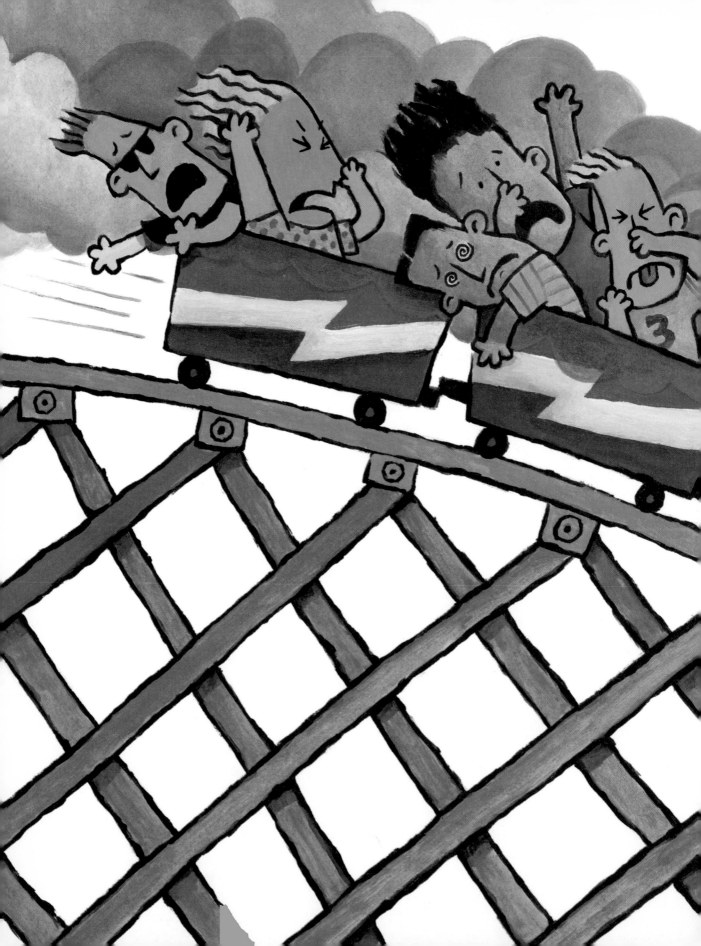

...but that idea stunk, too!

The plans to change Hally's bad
breath had failed. Now, only a
miracle could save Hally Tosis.
Sadly, the three friends said
good-night, unaware that a
miracle was just on the horizon.

Later that night, when everyone was sound asleep, two sneaky burglars crept into the Tosis house.
The two burglars were tiptoeing through the dark quiet rooms when suddenly they came upon Hally Tosis.

"Yikes," whispered one burglar. "It's a big, mean, scary dog!"
"Aw, don't be silly," whispered the other burglar. "That's only a cute, little, fuzzy puppy!"

The two burglars giggled at the sight
of such a friendly little dog.
"That dog couldn't hurt a fly,"
whispered one burglar.
"Come here, poochie poochie!"
whispered the other.
So Hally Tosis came over and gave
the burglars a nice big kiss.

The next morning, the Tosis family awoke
to find two burglars passed out cold
on their living room floor.

It was a miracle!

The Tosis family got a big reward
for turning in the crooks, and soon
Hally Tosis was the most famous
crime-fighting dog in the country.

In the end, Mr. and Mrs. Tosis changed their minds about finding a new home for Hally. They decided to keep their wonderful watchdog after all.

Because life without Hally Tosis
just wouldn't make any *scents!*